A Pony For Christmas

Bev Pettersen

Print ISBN: 978-1-987835-00-7
Westerhall Books

Editor: Pat Thomas
Cover Art Design: Kim Killion

http://www.BevPettersen.com

DEDICATION

To anyone who's ever wanted a horse for Christmas – with special thanks to the nieces: Tove, Bria, Kelly, Hanna and Liana. Thanks for the inspiration.

ALSO AVAILABLE FROM

BEV PETTERSEN AND WESTERHALL BOOKS

Jockeys and Jewels

Color My Horse

Fillies and Females

Thoroughbreds and Trailer Trash

Horses and Heroin

Studs and Stilettos

A Scandalous Husband

Repent (Novella)

CHAPTER ONE

Bragg Creek, Montana, 1961

Six-year-old Suzy Jenkins flattened against the snow, trying to make her body as small as possible. She peered across the frozen ground, her heart thumping, and checked the field for the bad boys.

Icy wind bit into her cheeks but she remained very still. This part of the walk home was the scariest. If they caught her in the open—away from the school ground—they'd pelt her with snowballs. Two of the boys couldn't throw well, but Jimmy, the tall boy with the black jacket, had excellent aim.

She wished Ruth Anne lived on this side of the fairgrounds too. It was more fun with a friend. Safer too. The boys always picked on children who walked alone. Ruth Anne said Suzy should tell the teacher, but when she tried that, Mrs. Roach only sniffed and said Santa Claus didn't like tattletales.

Suzy didn't think Santa Claus liked mean boys either, but just in case Mrs. Roach was right, she decided it was best not to complain. Christmas was only two weeks away and she didn't want to disappoint Santa.

The snow chilled her stomach, the cold seeping through her worn snowsuit, and she squirmed onto her side, trying to peer past the rusty dumpster. Movement flashed. She stiffened, even holding her breath so the boys wouldn't spot telltale white puffs.

But it was just Old Carl poking around the garbage. In the summer, the old man pushed a grocery cart filled with all sorts of treasures. However, in the winter he struggled through the snow, lugging a dark garbage bag. Suzy didn't think Carl liked winter much.

She glanced past him, still wary of the boys. There were two dismissal bells, and grades one to three were released before grade four. But the boys had long legs and they often caught up, especially if she stopped to play with Ruth Anne. The snow was wet today, and it had been easy to forget she was supposed to walk directly home. It had been too much fun building a snowman in Ruth Anne's yard.

Unfortunately this type of snow was also good for making snowballs.

She heard the boys before she saw them. It was the usual gang of three: Whitey who always had a runny nose, Peter who wasn't so bad and Jimmy, the tall boy. Jimmy was the meanest. When he looked at her with his little eyes, her stomach always felt funny.

She pressed harder against the snow, trying to turn invisible. Mrs. Roach had told them a story about a man in the war who had stayed so still, the bad soldiers never saw him. Suzy hoped the boys wouldn't see her either. Right now, they were yelling and wrestling, tumbling closer to Old Carl.

Carl didn't have a real home and slept in one of the deserted barns at the end of the fairgrounds. Some children were scared of him but she wasn't. Not much anyway. Her mother said it was mean to make fun of poor people and that everyone had a story. Then her eyes turned all sad, just like they did whenever she talked about their old town. Seeing her mother sad always made Suzy feel sad too.

She blew out a heavy sigh, then wiggled into a more comfortable position. Snowflakes fell faster, tickling her face. She wanted to brush them off but knew it was more important not to be seen.

However, it was difficult to lie still and she guessed she probably wouldn't be a good soldier. If only the boys would leave. She didn't mind walking past Carl. Sometimes he smelled funny but he always listened to her talk, and never once interrupted.

She raised her head a cautious inch and peeked over the hill. The boys weren't looking her way. Not yet. Jimmy straddled Whitey's back and was rubbing his face in the snow. Suzy hated face rubs. It wasn't bad when the snow was soft, but Jimmy sometimes held her down so long she couldn't breathe. One time he'd pushed her face into a lump of ice and it hurt so much she almost cried. She hoped he didn't hurt Whitey, but she was very relieved it wasn't her lying in the snow.

Someone yelled—Old Carl. He dropped his garbage bag and rushed toward the boys, waving his arms and hollering. Jimmy gave Whitey one last punch in the back of the head then scrambled to his feet. Whitey was probably glad the old man was around because even Jimmy had to listen to grownups. Jimmy stuck up his middle finger—the rude gesture Mrs. Roach hated—then followed Peter. The three boys ran across the field, leaving a line of footprints in the snow. They disappeared over the ridge.

Suzy sighed with relief. She rose, brushed the snow off her suit, then picked her way down the slope. This parking area belonged to the fairgrounds. But it wasn't used much, especially in the winter when it was mainly a dumping ground. Sometimes kids played here but other than Old Carl, it wasn't a place for grownups.

She trudged past Carl who was now stretching up on his toes and poking in the dumpster. His jacket was ripped and the tips of his ears were beet red.

She tugged her hat lower, relieved her ears weren't sticking out like that. But she was also cold. Snow trickled down the inside of her jacket, chilling the back of her neck. Luckily it was Friday. Her mother sometimes made hot chocolate on Fridays, and nothing warmed her up better than that.

She waved at Carl but didn't stop to talk and hurried the rest of the way home. Her mother was always happier on Fridays because she didn't have to work on weekends, and it was their special time to be together.

The door opened before Suzy could lift the mat and search for the key.

"Why are you late?" her mother asked, frowning. "The McDonald girls have been home for an hour."

Suzy kicked off her boots, not speaking. The main reason she was late was because of the bullies, but everyone said Santa didn't like tattletales. And he was probably listening. He even saw children when they were sleeping, although that wasn't particularly worrisome. Suzy was very good when she slept.

"Guess what?" she said quickly. "The new boy pulled Ruth Anne's hair. Mrs. Roach was cross and said that if he couldn't behave, he should move back to his old town."

"Poor boy," her mother said. "It's hard to move to a new school, a new home. But you like it here now, right?"

Suzy nodded. She could barely remember her old house, except that it had been a lot bigger.

"That's good." Her mother shook the snow off Suzy's jacket and hung it by the heater. "There's hot chocolate in the kitchen, and I picked up a bag of sugar so we can make cookies."

Suzy squealed in delight and rushed into the kitchen. "Can we cut them in the shape of a Christmas tree?" she called over her shoulder. "And can I take one to school tomorrow for Ruth Anne?"

"Sure, that would be nice," her mother said, walking past the oven and pulling the flour from the cupboard.

"Maybe I should take one to the teacher too," Suzy added. "Maybe even everyone in my class. Would that be nice enough?"

"Nice enough? What do you mean?"

Suzy dragged a chair closer to the table. Mrs. Roach said Santa Claus was always watching, even in the summer, but Suzy thought it made sense to be extra nice just before Christmas. There were a lot of children in her class though. And they would eat a lot of cookies, maybe all of them. However, she wanted Santa to remember her. And her pony.

She'd been preparing for a pony for a long time, and everything was ready now. Their little yard already had a picket fence and a shed. She'd even found two buckets by the dumpster. One of them was cracked, but the other one only had a broken handle so it would be perfect for water. At first she thought Carl might need the buckets, but he'd only kicked them aside, so she'd scooped them up and carefully placed them in her shed.

She had two carrots in the shed as well, taken from the bag in the fridge that her mother used to make stew. They were a little brown and shriveled, after waiting so long at the bottom of the bucket, but when summer came she'd be able to climb the tree by the fairgrounds and pick fresh apples.

Her library book said ponies liked apples and carrots but that they really only needed grass and water. And luckily the grass in their yard grew very long. They didn't own a lawnmower so the new pony would surely make her mother happy too.

But not as happy as Suzy. She'd wanted a pony for as long as she could remember, even before Ruth Anne's birthday last winter.

"What do you mean by nice enough?" her mother repeated, pulling back Suzy's attention.

"You know," Suzy said. "Nice enough for Santa."

Her mother smiled and tied the strings on Suzy's apron. "Is that why you cleaned your room last week? And why you haven't been asking to stay up late?"

Suzy jammed her lips together and reached across the table for the bowl. She'd also been good in other ways, and it was disappointing her mother didn't notice that she now brushed her teeth without being asked.

"You still want a skipping rope for Christmas, right?" Her mother paused, dipping her head so she could see Suzy's face. "Are you sure that's what you want? Not a different kind of toy, maybe a doll?"

Suzy wrinkled her nose. "I don't like dolls," she muttered. Sometimes her mother forgot the most important things. She was always worrying about her job, and the little line on her forehead seemed to be getting bigger. Other than that, Suzy's mother was the prettiest and nicest lady in town, maybe even the whole world. But there was no sense asking *her* for a pony.

"We can't afford one," she'd said last summer. And her voice had turned so sharp, Suzy had never asked again.

But Santa was different. He brought boys and girls all sorts of things. Ruth Anne said it was important to mail a letter instead of leaving it by the fireplace. That way he remembered everything and wouldn't get any presents mixed up. It seemed to work because nobody received more presents than Ruth Anne.

And this year Suzy's entire school had mailed their letters. Now that Suzy was six she could print a lot of words—Mrs. Roach said she was one of the best printers in the class. And Suzy was going to leave milk and cookies too, like Ruth Anne always did.

"What do you think are Santa's favorite cookies?" she asked.

"These ones," her mother said, ruffling Suzy's hair. "And he likes them cut in the shape of a Christmas tree too."

Suzy blew out a satisfied sigh. She'd make sure she saved at least three cookies. Santa might want more than one.

"Your teacher called today," her mother said.

"Mrs. Roach?" Suzy's voice quavered.

"Yes. She asked if some older boys were bothering you. Is everything okay?"

Suzy blew out a relieved breath, glad Mrs. Roach hadn't told her mother she was a tattletale. Her mother didn't like tattling either. And both Suzy and Ruth Anne agreed that tattletales were almost as bad as bullies.

"Everything is good," Suzy said, unable to resist dipping her finger into the sugar. She turned her head away, then licked the sweetness from the tip of her finger, squeezing her eyes shut in delight.

Sugar was so good. Maybe she could put some in her pony's bucket. Not much, just a sprinkle to shake over the carrots. Her mother wouldn't want her to take a lot, but it would be nice to have something special on her pony's very first day. It would be hard to carry in her hand though...

"Could we get some sugar cubes for Christmas?" Suzy asked. "Ruth Anne's mother has some in a silver bowl on her table, and she let me have one once. You could even put them in your coffee."

Her mother gave a tight smile.

"I'm not getting big ideas," Suzy added quickly, wishing she could remember not to talk so much about Ruth Anne's house. Her mother always smiled and listened, but it was a tired smile, the kind where the corners of her mouth went up but her eyes stayed sad. Not like the wedding picture on the mantle where she was laughing at Suzy's father and her eyes were all sparkly and her face glowed.

"Maybe we'll get some sugar lumps if you're extra good," Suzy's mother said. "And don't put your finger back in the bowl."

Suzy guiltily pulled her hand back. Her mother was better than Mrs. Roach at noticing things. Maybe even as good as Santa.

She picked up the wooden spoon, impatiently waiting for her mother to measure the flour. "Ruth Anne's mother made sugar cookies for the fair tomorrow. There's going to be a big horse race, the kind where they pull sleds."

"Sulkies," her mother said, so quietly Suzy could barely hear.

Suzy nodded. "We went to a fair before, right? Before Daddy had sumption?"

"Consumption."

"That's what I said." Suzy stuck the spoon in the bowl and tried to stir, but it tipped and flour spilled over the counter. She froze in dismay. Her mother didn't like to waste food, and probably Santa didn't like it much either.

But her mother didn't scold. She had a faraway look in her eyes and Suzy could tell she was thinking of something else. Suzy could barely remember her father, but it was clear her mother did.

"Can we go to the fair tomorrow?" Suzy asked, struggling to scoop up the spilled flour with the big spoon. "Everyone is going, and Ruth Anne said last year you were allowed to pat a horse."

"Okay," her mother said.

"And it's free," Suzy went on. "At Christmas time Mr. Barrett pays for everything." Her spoon tipped in midair. "We can go?" She blinked in amazement.

Her mother had never been to Mr. Barrett's party. Last year Suzy had been the only girl in her class, probably the whole school, who didn't go. Ruth Anne said there were free candy canes and Christmas music. Suzy didn't mind missing the music but she loved candy canes. And horses. Next to ponies, horses were the best thing in the world.

"Yes," her mother said, turning toward the sink. "You deserve it. And maybe for Christmas you can draw me a picture of a racehorse. I'd love that. We can hang it on the fridge with your other pictures."

Suzy gave a happy nod and began to hum. She'd certainly draw her mother another horse picture. But it wasn't really necessary. Because this year Santa Claus was going to bring them a real live pony.

CHAPTER TWO

Suzy gripped her mother's hand, slightly awed by the crowd of surging people. Everyone was talking and laughing, and the huge building smelled like cinnamon and coffee and cigarettes. There were more legs than she could count.

The men had jackets and big winter boots but most women wore dresses and high heels. At the far end a group of grownups sang *Jingle Bells*, but Suzy could barely hear the words. She didn't see any candy canes or horses either.

"The racehorses are outside on the track," her mother said, as if reading her mind. "This is the clubhouse, the south entrance to the fairgrounds."

Suzy peered through the glass windows toward the track. It looked way more fun outside. Children were running and playing, and even mean Jimmy was smiling. He must have taken someone's candy cane because he had two gripped in his hand.

She tugged at her lower lip. It was mainly big children out there and she didn't even see

Ruth Anne. But there were several men outside too, all crowded around Mr. Barrett and his black cowboy hat.

Ruth Anne said Mr. Barrett owned the town but Suzy's mother said he owned a ranch. Suzy didn't know what he owned. But he always looked very stern, and she was quite certain nobody would dare to be bad around him. Not even Jimmy.

She tugged her hand loose. "Can I go outside and play?"

"Yes," her mother said, glancing toward the track. "But put your hat and mittens back on. And don't scare the horses."

Suzy sighed. She wasn't going to scare any horses. But she wanted to escape before the grownups came. Mr. Joudrey always pinched her cheek and talked about taking them to a movie, even though her mother was always busy. And Mrs. Smith wore too much perfume and kept talking about how it was such a shame Suzy's mother always looked so tired.

"I'll be right here by the coat rack," her mother said. "Remember your manners."

Suzy nodded and dodged through the maze of people toward the tall windows. A big door led to the outside. But it was heavy and even using both hands, she couldn't pull it open.

"It slides, stupid."

Suzy turned toward the voice. Whitey and Peter loomed behind her. Whitey's nose was red and runny, and it looked like Jimmy had been rubbing his face in the snow again.

She scowled at Whitey. "I'm not stupid," she said.

Whitey just shoved her aside, slid the door open and rushed outside.

Peter, however, paused. "The first time I came here," he said, "I didn't know it slid either."

He pushed the door further back and pointed at the group of men. "The man with the sheepskin jacket—the one with the black cowboy hat—that's Mr. Barrett. He has the candy canes in a box. Just tell him you didn't get yours yet."

Peter pulled his hat further over his face, acting like he was embarrassed. He ran off in Whitey's direction before she could tell him that everyone knew who Mr. Barrett was.

She followed Peter outside but hesitated in front of the glass door. The wind was blowing but it wasn't at all cold. Sunshine warmed the air and she probably didn't need her mittens. It would be easier to eat the candy cane if her hands were bare. But first she needed to get one.

The men stood by the rail, not paying any attention to the children. There was a red box by their feet but they seemed to be talking about something important. The tall man, Mr. Barrett, looked impatient.

She edged closer, knowing she couldn't interrupt. However, her mouth watered simply imagining the taste of peppermint. A short man with a striped tie was talking now, waving his arm and gesturing at the barns. As soon as he stopped speaking, she'd ask for her candy cane. It wasn't really interrupting, not if no one was talking. And she'd be sure to use her best manners.

She checked over her shoulder. It was doubtful Jimmy had remembered to say 'please' or 'thank you.' So if Santa was watching, she'd seem extra good.

The men's voices rose as she sidled closer.

"I know you don't like to talk about this," the short man said, "but we need that last barn for horses. It's a waste of twenty good stalls."

Mr. Barrett crossed his arms. "The barn stays empty. If necessary, I'll build another." His voice was scary firm, like Mrs. Roach's when she told Suzy not to talk.

"But it's tough living like that," another man said. "Can't you talk to him? Persuade him to move?"

Mr. Barrett shook his head. "He doesn't speak to anyone. Certainly not to me."

"But this is crazy. Carl's been sleeping on the fairgrounds for five years. He's not going to change. The kindest thing would be to have him committed. At least then he'd have a bath and a decent meal—"

"Enough," Mr. Barrett snapped. All the men turned silent, even the man with the tie.

Suzy tugged at her lower lip. For some reason, Mr. Barrett reminded her of Mrs. Roach, even though he was much bigger. And younger. And she was quite certain they were talking about Old Carl. He was the only man she knew who lived in a barn.

It was sad Carl didn't get any decent meals. He wasn't even very polite so Santa Claus probably wouldn't bring him a present. But Mr. Barrett was wrong about one thing.

Because Carl did speak.

He always yelled at the bad boys, and once he'd told her to get off the track because a train was coming. And there was that time the boys pushed her down and he thought she was crying—even though she wasn't. He'd helped her up and brushed the snow from her face. Ruth Anne wasn't allowed to talk to Carl, but Suzy was glad her mother hadn't said that.

The men were still silent so she stepped forward and tugged at Mr. Barrett's sleeve.

"Hi," she said, "I'm Suzy Jenkins. Thank you very much for the nice Christmas party. Could I have a candy cane, please?"

He looked down with eyes so blue they reminded her of the sky. And for a moment she was afraid she hadn't remembered her good manners after all. Because he just stared. Then he bent down and shook her hand, and his smile was so nice she wasn't afraid at all.

"Hello, Suzy Jenkins," he said. His voice lowered. "You're the first person who's thanked me," he whispered. "So thank *you.*" He reached into the box and passed her a candy cane. "You come back after the race is over. If any candy canes are left, you can have them all. Okay?"

She nodded. "Okay," she whispered back.

She wanted to ask how many were left in the box but he'd already turned to talk to a man with a notebook. And it wasn't good to be greedy. But she gripped her candy cane in her mitten and skipped with delight.

Maybe she'd even end up with three candy canes, one more than Jimmy. She could eat this one now, and still have two for Christmas. Santa Claus wouldn't give her any candy, not when he was already bringing a pony. And her mother said she couldn't ask for more than one thing.

She tugged off her mittens and admired the candy cane. It was red and white and thicker than her finger. She stuck the end in her mouth, closing her eyes in bliss. If she sucked it slowly, with no biting, it might last all afternoon.

"I wish Carl would leave," came a man's low voice. "No one wants him here."

Suzy opened her eyes and looked up, but the short man with the tie wasn't talking to her. In fact, the two men didn't seem to notice her.

"Some day he's going to starve to death and Barrett will find him frozen in the snow. He'll wish he listened then."

Suzy stiffened, the candy cane still in her mouth. *She* didn't want Carl to leave. The boys weren't so mean when a grownup was around. But she didn't want Carl to starve to death either.

She thought for a moment. Then pulled the candy cane from her mouth and carefully stuck it in her jacket pocket. She'd give it to Carl on Monday, when she saw him after school. That would give him something good to eat so he wouldn't starve. Besides, she was going to get more candy canes later.

She shot an anxious look at the box by Mr. Barrett's boots and then checked the front entrance. There didn't seem to be any new children arriving. It was mainly adults inside. Most of them had taken off their coats. They were talking and laughing, and even from here, she could see that Mr. Joudrey's face was unusually red. It didn't look like any of the grownups would want a candy cane either; they were all holding glasses.

She strained to see her mother's golden hair. There she was, standing in the corner. She hadn't taken off her coat and it looked like she wanted to leave.

Suzy's heart sank. She edged to the other side of the laughing children. It wasn't time to go yet. She didn't want to miss the race and Ruth Anne said that last year they were allowed to pat a horse. And Mr. Barrett had told her to wait until the end to see if there were any extra candy canes.

She gripped the rail and stood very still, trying to stay out of her mother's sight.

Peter poked her in the ribs. "Did you see the Standardbreds warming up?" he asked.

Suzy gave him a suspicious look. His mouth was streaked red from candy cane and he'd unbuttoned his jacket. He didn't even wear a hat or mittens. But he didn't look mean.

She shrugged. She knew Standardbreds were a kind of horse, much bigger than a pony, and when they raced they pulled a little wagon. Sulky, her mother had called it.

"Standardbreds are tough," Peter added importantly. "They can race in the winter, not like Thoroughbreds. My dad says Mr. Barrett's horses always win, no matter what type of race."

Suzy stared over the snow-covered track. It looked like horses were coming. She could see their heads and brightly colored numbers. "I see them warming up now," she said, her voice rising with excitement.

"It's the start of the race, stupid," Peter said. "It's a half mile track so they go around twice." But he smiled when he spoke, and she didn't really mind that he called her 'stupid,' not like when Whitey said it.

She stretched on her toes, trying to see over the rail. Now the horses were lined right in front of her. They were huge, all black and brown with big heads and streaming tails and colorful cloths on their backs. Men sat in little seats close to the horses' tails and goggles covered the drivers' faces. She gripped the rail, quivering with excitement. But then, much too quickly, they were gone.

"The race just started," Peter said, matter-of-factly. "But they'll come around again. Who do you think will win?"

"I don't know," she said, squinting up the track, trying to see what was happening. The horses were strung out now, their feet kicking up clumps of snow. One horse was way ahead and white puffs shot from his nose.

"Just pick a number," Peter said impatiently. "I pick number two, that's Mr. Barrett's horse."

Suzy tugged at her lip. Number six was her favorite because for her last birthday her mother had made a chocolate cake with thick icing on the top. It even had extra icing on the sides. "I pick number six," she said.

"Okay," Peter said. "Your horse is in front."

And then the horses passed by again and she couldn't stop smiling because Peter was right, and number six was the fast horse in front.

"But that's only half the race," Peter said. "They have to run around one more time."

She nodded. For a boy, Peter was quite smart.

There were a lot of grownups standing by the rail now, and they were all yelling and cheering and it was very exciting. Especially since number six was winning.

But then it seemed like he slowed. All the other horses passed him and number two was in front now, running down the middle of the track, so fast the ground shook.

"I won!" Peter said, jumping up and down, and grinning like an idiot.

Suzy gave a little sniff. Her horse had sort of won because he'd been in front most of the way. Maybe he didn't know the race was so long. When she had her pony, she wasn't going to make him run far. Besides, it would be more fun to ride a horse than drive it.

"When do we get to pat the horse?" she asked.

"In the winner's circle," Peter said over his shoulder. "This way."

She didn't see a circle but she was too small to see over all the people, so she followed Peter as he darted around the grownups' legs. He led her to a gate where a man in a blue uniform blocked the way. A group of children had already gathered there, including Ruth Anne. She wore her fancy church coat with the black buttons and her hands were stuck in a fur-lined muff. When she saw Suzy, she pulled out her fingers and waved.

Her mother grabbed Ruth Anne's hand. "Move to the front," she said. It wasn't a soft whisper but loud and bossy.

"But I want to stand by Suzy," Ruth Anne said, twisting around.

"She's not a club member," her mother said. "She's not allowed in." She pulled Ruth Anne past the guard and through the little gate, then pushed her in line with several other children.

Suzy pressed her face against the steel rails, longingly watching the children on the other side of the gate. A man picked them up, one at a time, and let them pat the brown horse's neck. The horse had number two on the top of his head and also a bright cloth on his back. Some of the kids in line with Ruth Anne were crying and afraid but Suzy knew she wouldn't have been scared, and she gave a wistful sigh.

Peter wasn't allowed in either, but he'd found a good spot on top of a garbage can where he could reach over the gate and touch the horse's back. The guard yelled at him and Peter scrambled down but he was pumping his fist and grinning. And no wonder—he'd patted a real live racehorse!

He ran up to Suzy. "Did you see me touch the horse?" he asked, still grinning.

Suzy nodded.

"Jimmy and Whitey don't like horses," Peter said. "But I do."

"Me too," Suzy said. "When I get my pony I'll let you pat him. But not Jimmy."

"You're getting a pony?" Peter's eyes widened.

Suzy nodded. "Santa's bringing me one for Christmas."

"But you can't afford a pony. Nobody in our neighborhood has one."

"That's because they didn't ask Santa."

"But it's not just getting them," Peter said. "My dad says they cost too much to feed."

Suzy sighed. "Did you ever ask for one?"

"No, because that's just stupid. Santa can't bring a pony."

"Well, he's bringing me one." She clenched the insides of her mittens and edged away, deciding she didn't want to talk to Peter anymore.

She pressed her nose against another section of the cold fence and continued watching the children on the other side of the gate.

Now it was Ruth Anne's turn to pat the horse. However, he lifted his tail and pooped, and

Ruth Anne squealed and plugged her nose, and all the men laughed.

And then Mr. Barrett put a blanket over the horse and gestured toward the barns, and a smiling man with dark skin led the horse away. And even though everyone looked happy, Suzy's chest ached.

"Are you having fun?" Suzy's mother asked.

Suzy turned around and tried to smile at her mom but for some reason her mouth stuck.

"You must be cold after being outside all this time," her mother said. "Want to warm up before we walk home?"

"We can't go yet," Suzy said. "Mr. Barrett might have extra candy canes. He told me to stay until it was over."

"Mr. Barrett?" Her mother blinked and glanced over Suzy's head. "But he's a busy man. You can't bother him about something like that."

"It's no bother. He has them in a box, and he said I could have the leftovers."

"We're not accepting any more charity," her mother said. "He already sponsored this Christmas party. It's greedy to ask for more."

"But I didn't ask," Suzy said stubbornly. "He offered. And the race is over and everyone's leaving now. Look, there are still some candy canes in the box."

"Okay," her mother said slowly. "Five more minutes." And then she smiled. But it was one of those tight smiles and her eyes looked sad, and it was clear she wasn't happy about staying.

Suzy glanced over the rail. She wished Mr. Barrett would come back before her mother turned impatient and made her leave. But he was still in the winner's circle, on the other side of the gate, talking to a man with a camera.

She edged closer to the candy cane box. The top was open and she peered in, then gave a little hop of excitement. There were at least five candy canes left—maybe even six.

But the man with the tie gave her an odd look. He scooped up the box and passed it to a dark-haired woman who looked like she'd just eaten something sour. "We better take these home," he said, "before the ragamuffins steal them."

Suzy's face turned warm. But the man with the tie didn't look at her again. He and the woman turned and walked out the clubhouse door, carrying the candy cane box.

Her candy cane box.

Suzy's eyes itched. She rubbed at her eyes, but the wool in her mittens only made them itch more.

And then her mother was kneeling beside her, and her face looked so concerned, Suzy's eyes hurt even worse. "What's wrong, sweetie?" her mother asked.

Suzy ducked her head against her mother's warm coat and sniffed. "This isn't a very fun party," she said.

"We'll go home now," her mother said. "And after supper we'll make some popcorn and decorate the Christmas tree. If you want, you can invite the McDonald girls over."

"But they're too big to play with." She pulled away, still sniffing. "And I didn't even get to pat the horse."

"Did you want to pat a horse?" a man's deep voice asked.

She looked up, past his long legs and thick sheepskin jacket, all the way up to Mr. Barrett's face. He sounded a little annoyed. But he wasn't looking at her. He was frowning at the guard by the steel gate. "I didn't want to do it that way," he said.

And then he surprised her. He knelt down in the snow, beside her and her mother and a squashed cigarette box. "How could we make this party better?" he asked. "Would most children want to pat a horse? Or maybe next year they'd like a sleigh ride?"

And then he waited for her to answer, and it was hard to talk because he was watching as if she were an adult and even though his hat was so big, his eyes were patient and kind.

But her mother interrupted. “The party was very nice,” she said hastily. “And we’re both appreciative. Thank you.”

Mr. Barrett’s black hat turned, and he looked at her mother. And then he smiled. “You’re Caroline who works in Joudrey’s store. I’m Jake.”

“Yes, I know,” she said, and her cheeks turned all red, and she and Mr. Barrett just stared at each other, and they seemed to forget about making the party better.

“The children would like a sleigh ride,” Suzy said firmly.

Mr. Barrett looked back at her, his eyes smiling. “All right,” he said. “But we can’t let you and your mother go home this year without patting a horse.”

“No,” Suzy said, trying not to grin. But he wasn’t looking at her anymore. He and her mother were staring at each other again. And Suzy was a little afraid he might get busy and forget, like he had with the candy canes.

“Where is the horse I can pat?” she asked.

“Over at the barn,” he said, holding out his arm to her mother and helping her rise.

“We can walk over there now,” he added, glancing down at her mother’s black boots. “You’re one of the few women who wore sensible shoes.”

"Those are Mommy's fancy boots," Suzy said. "They look nice but there's a hole in the back. But I can help her walk around the deep snow."

Mr. Barrett's mouth twitched. "We'll both help her," he said.

CHAPTER THREE

Suzy held out another handful of hay, delighted how the horse's velvety mouth tickled her fingers. His eyes were big and brown, and his lips scrunched up when he chewed. And she thought this was probably the best day of her life.

Mr. Barrett said she could feed the horse as much hay as he'd eat and that he was the gentlest animal in the barn. She wasn't allowed to go near any of the other horses though, even when they stuck their heads over the stall doors and she could tell they wanted some hay too.

Her mother was further down the aisle, drinking coffee with Mr. Barrett. She kept looking at Suzy, but it seemed like she wasn't so impatient to leave now. Suzy hoped they would just keep talking. She'd be happy to stay here until suppertime. And on Monday she could tell Ruth Anne all about the barn at the fairgrounds.

Everything smelled of hay and horse, and it was all perfectly wonderful. There were more horses than she could count and it was clean and tidy—not like the barn in her library book. Shiny leather harnesses hung on the wall, and there was even a place at the end where they kept the sulkies. And the buckets were the same kind as the ones she had for her pony.

There was a lot of hay stacked in the corner. And no wonder because this brown horse ate very fast. He was tall too. When he lifted his head, she couldn't reach his nose. She rose on her tiptoes, trying to see over the stall door but it was way too high.

She frowned. It was probably a good thing she wasn't getting a big horse. She couldn't even pronounce this horse's name. It was double words, like Ruth Anne's, but much longer. She was going to call her pony a short name. King or Brownie or possibly even Blackie. Unless he was two colors like the mayor's pony. She wrinkled her nose, but couldn't think of any name that would fit a two-colored pony.

"Is everything okay?" a man asked. He wore big overalls and pushed a green wheelbarrow, and even though he didn't have any front teeth it looked like he smiled a lot. "Did that horse scare you?"

She shook her head and patted the horse again, just to show the man she wasn't scared.

"Boss thought you might be getting bored. Is that your mother with him?"

Suzy nodded.

"She sure is pretty. Does she like horses too?" The man set down the wheelbarrow, his head tilting. "I just wonder because I've never seen Boss bring a woman back here. Not unless they were buying a horse. And he told me to make sure you were having a good time."

Suzy opened her mouth to say she was having a wonderful time—the best time of her life—but the man kept talking.

"There's a cat in the empty stall by the office," he said. "Your mom might be less inclined to leave if you weren't playing so close to a big horse. *We* know he's gentle but you know how mothers worry." He gave a little wink.

Suzy nodded. It was sad to stop patting the horse but her mother did tend to worry. She wouldn't fret over a cat though. And Suzy would still be able to sit in the barn and watch the horses stick their heads over the doors.

She followed the man down the aisle. Her mother didn't seem so concerned now. She smiled at Suzy and then back at Mr. Barrett.

Suzy squared her shoulders and walked behind the man pushing the wheelbarrow, making sure she didn't run and trying to use her best manners.

"Maybe you'd like to go outside and see the goat too, Suzy," Mr. Barrett called. "He's black and white. We call him Oreo."

Oreo. Suzy glanced back at Mr. Barrett and grinned. If Santa brought her a black and white pony, Oreo would be an excellent name.

"Don't forget to put your hat on," her mother called.

The man with the wheelbarrow stopped and waited for Suzy to pull on her hat. "Guess we'll go outside and see Oreo first," he said cheerfully. "I think Boss is quite smitten. It's good to see him smile again."

Suzy thought it was good to see her mother smile again too, especially since her eyes hadn't looked happy at the party. Maybe she was starting to like horses too.

Suzy stepped outside the barn then stopped and gawked with disbelief. The sun was shining in her eyes, but she could still see that there were more barns like this one. And there were many more horses too, more than she'd ever thought possible.

Heads stuck over stall doors everywhere. One of the horses was even white. The hair on her neck was long and fluffy, and she looked so pretty, and Suzy wanted to pat them all.

"Are those Mr. Barrett's horses too?" she asked, spinning in delight.

"No, those belong to other people." The man dumped the wheelbarrow into a big pile full of stained brown straw. "Mr. Barrett has more horses at his ranch outside of town. But he only keeps the ones he's racing here. In the spring, the barns will be full of Thoroughbreds and Quarter Horses, and these Standardbreds will go home."

"Are there any ponies here?" She peered hopefully down the long row of barns.

The man chuckled. "Nope. Ponies are a waste of money. No better than a big dog, except they eat more and are way too expensive."

Suzy crossed her arms. Her mother had said almost the same thing. "But they eat grass," she said. "And grass is free."

"Grass doesn't grow in the winter," the man said. "And hay is expensive, especially after the drought this year."

He kept talking but Suzy's mind was whirling too much to listen. Maybe she should ask Santa for hay too. But then that would be two presents, and her mother didn't like her to be greedy.

"There's our goat." The man pointed at the alleyway between the two barns. "He wanders loose around the backside, but no one ever complains. He and Carl are the boss's albatross."

Suzy stared at the black and white goat and stopped worrying about hay. Santa would figure it out. Mrs. Roach said he always knew what to bring children. And she didn't know what an albatross was, but the goat looked very cute. He had two curly horns and was almost as big as a pony.

"May I pat him, please?" she asked.

"Sure. He might try to chew your mittens but he's very friendly."

Suzy pulled off her red mittens and tucked them in her pocket. They were her good mittens and her mother would be sad if anything chewed them. Once a mouse had ruined Suzy's winter jacket and her mother had cried. Suzy didn't like it when her mother cried.

She hurried toward the goat. He was chewing something, and turned his head away, as if afraid she might take it.

"Hi, Oreo." She reached out and touched his neck. His hair was rougher than a horse's but he was smaller and easier to reach. She slipped her hand around one of his hard horns, guessing it probably felt a lot like a reindeer's.

His eyes were brown and his mouth moved as he chewed. But it looked like he was eating a dirty rag which didn't seem at all healthy. When Ruth Anne's dog had swallowed a sock, he'd been very sick.

Suzy glanced back at the man with the wheelbarrow but he'd already walked back inside the barn. She reached for the rag, trying to tug it from the goat's mouth. But he only yanked his head away and wandered further between the barns. She sped up, trying to circle in front of him, but he began to trot.

She laughed and ran faster. Oreo sped up, but not too much, and he seemed to be having fun too. It was a great game of tag, until he abruptly dashed down another alley and into a creepy barn.

She paused, not sure at first why the building looked so lonely, and rather scary. Then she realized—this barn was deserted. Not a single horse peered out over a stall door.

"Oreo," she called, wishing he'd come back.

She edged closer, straining to see into the shadows. Nothing moved in the aisle. But just inside the doorway there were several open boxes filled with store-bought clothes. She could still see the price tags. And one of the boxes was filled with cans of food. However, everything was covered with a thin film of snow, as if it had sat there for a very long time.

Suzy blinked. There was something else in the aisle. It looked like a wooden cross, like the kind at church except it was surrounded by dead flowers.

She backed up, her throat drying. She didn't want to leave Oreo in the spooky barn but she didn't want to stay here any longer. Maybe this was a ghost barn and even though it looked deserted there were people inside. Ghost people who didn't need food or clothes. And maybe the ghost people were looking at her right now, but she couldn't see them.

"There you are."

She wheeled toward the voice, relieved to see the nice man who pushed the wheelbarrow.

"Better come away from there," he called. "Carl doesn't appreciate visitors. Doesn't appreciate anything," he added, shooting a dark look at the boxes.

"Is this where Carl lives?" she asked, breathing a little easier. She knew for a fact Carl was no ghost.

The man nodded. "Five years now. Ever since his daughter hit her head on that doorway."

Suzy peered up at the doorsill. "She must have been very tall."

"Runaway horse," the man said with a smile. "That's why Boss always has us lead his horses to the track now. Come on. He wants to drive you and your mother home."

"But we can walk," Suzy said. "We always walk."

"Not today," the man said.

CHAPTER FOUR

"Did you really go to the backside?" Peter asked, his eyes widening.

Suzy nodded, glad someone was finally showing the proper enthusiasm. At school today, Ruth Anne had barely listened, not even seeming to care about the horses.

"I patted a goat too," Suzy added. "His name was Oreo and he liked to play. But after a while he ran away."

"Were you in Mr. Barrett's barn with all his racehorses?" Peter scooped up a handful of snow, clearly more interested in horses than goats. "Did you see where Old Carl lives? And the cross he keeps for his daughter?"

She nodded, warily eyeing the snow in Peter's hands. She didn't think he'd throw it at her, especially since Whitey and Jimmy had already disappeared over the hill. But it was Monday. And boys were always wilder after a weekend.

Peter pulled back his arm and whipped the

snowball at the dumpster. "I wish I could have seen the barns," he said. "And where his daughter was killed. My dad says Carl stopped liking horses the day she died, and that girls aren't strong enough to ride Thoroughbreds anyway. But I'm strong. And I'll never let any horse run back to the barn."

"Me neither," Suzy said. But she was glad ponies were small. There'd never be any danger of hitting her head on a door. "Maybe I'll let you ride my pony," she said.

"Don't be stupid," Peter said. "You're not really getting a pony...are you?"

She nodded. She wanted to say that maybe if he were better behaved, he could ask for a pony too. But just today Mrs. Roach had yelled at Peter and Jimmy. Suzy had seen them in the principal's office, heads ducked, hands stuck in their pockets. Ruth Anne said they were getting the strap. And Christmas was only five days away.

"You can ride my pony," she said, "and then you can practice not hitting your head."

"Okay." Peter scooped up another handful of snow. "But I'll believe it when I see it."

He tossed the snow at her, but it was a halfhearted gesture and the snowball fell harmlessly at her feet. He grinned and ran over the hill, following Jimmy's and Whitey's tracks.

Suzy tugged her hat lower, wishing Peter had stayed by the dumpster while she waited for

Carl. It was almost supper time, and she was cold and hungry. But Carl still hadn't appeared. She patted her pocket, checking for the candy cane. Maybe she didn't *have* to give it to him.

Even Santa would understand it was hard to share when she just had one. On the other hand, she'd been to a Christmas party and seen a race and even patted a real horse. Carl lived in a shadowy barn with only a cross, and maybe ghosts.

She wiggled with indecision. Her mother would be home from work soon, and she didn't like it when Suzy dawdled.

"Did those boys hurt you again? Are you afraid to walk home?"

Suzy turned. Carl stood only ten feet away. He had a garbage bag slung over his shoulder and he frowned so deeply his bushy eyebrows almost touched.

"No." Suzy pulled out the candy cane. "I just stayed so I could give you this. I got it at the big party on Saturday. I only licked it for a minute."

He stared at the candy cane gripped in her mitten.

"Why would I want that?" he finally asked.

"Because you don't have one, and I wanted to share." She shuffled her feet, but his eyes were so blue it was impossible to not tell the truth. "And Santa's watching," she admitted. "So I'm trying to be extra good."

Carl didn't speak, but he lowered the garbage bag and placed it in the snow. "Of course," he finally said. "It's Christmas time. I'd forgotten this is when children have to be good."

She gave a solemn nod, glad he understood.

"But you must know lots of other people who would like a candy cane," he said.

"I wanted you to have it," she said. "So you wouldn't starve."

Carl coughed and covered his mouth. "Well, that's very nice of you," he said, lowering his hand. "I haven't had a candy cane for a long time."

"They taste good," Suzy said. "And if you lick it slow, it will last all day."

She tried to pass him the candy cane but it stuck on her mitten, and it took a moment to pull free. When she finally tugged it loose, the candy cane was covered with blue from her pocket, along with red wool from her mitten.

"Oh, no." She stared in dismay at the ruined candy cane.

"It looks delicious," Carl said gruffly. He took the candy cane, not seeming to mind that it was covered in pieces of wool. He had a big smile on his face and he stuck the end right in his mouth.

"You can bite it if you want," she said, glad now that she had saved it for him.

"No. I'll eat it slow...so Santa is sure to see."

Suzy nodded her approval. "Good idea," she said.

CHAPTER FIVE

"What did I tell you about coming straight home?" Suzy's mother frowned and helped unzip her jacket. "Were you playing with Ruth Anne again?"

"No," Suzy said. She turned her head and sniffed. Something smelled delicious, like chocolate. "Are you making fudge?" she asked hopefully.

"Yes, but it's for Mrs. McDonald. For watching out for you after school. And because it's Christmas."

Suzy sighed, wishing the fudge was for them and not the McDonalds. "Can I lick the bowl?" she asked.

"Suzy," her mother said in a firm voice. "Where were you for the last hour?"

"Waiting for Carl." She crossed her fingers and stared down at her wet socks. Some parents told their children to stay away from Carl, but she couldn't exactly remember what her mother had said.

"The homeless man?" Her mother tilted Suzy's head, forcing her to look up. "Why were you waiting for him?"

"Because I wanted to give him my candy cane," Suzy said. "From the Christmas party."

"Oh." Her mother was quiet for a moment. "That was nice of you."

Suzy breathed a sigh of relief. Her mother always said it was important to be nice, to everyone. But Ruth Anne's mother said that too, and she sometimes wasn't nice at all. "Some men at the party said Carl should be committed," Suzy said. "What does that mean?"

Her mother bent down and placed Suzy's boots by the heater. "It just means they don't understand him."

"Peter said Carl lives in a barn because his daughter hit her head and died. But she was on a horse," Suzy added quickly. "Not a pony."

"I don't know much about Carl," her mother said, "but Mrs. McDonald says he's harmless. Sometimes when people are sad, they just like to be left alone."

"But you're not sad anymore, are you?"

"No." She gave Suzy a hug. "You make me very happy."

"That's good," Suzy said, even though she wished her mother's eyes would sparkle again. "And remember Mr. Barrett said that after

Christmas he was coming to town and taking us for dinner."

"I haven't forgotten," her mother said, still holding Suzy's shoulders. "Do you like Mr. Barrett?"

Suzy nodded. He was way nicer than Mr. Joudrey. And his truck had a nice leathery smell and it even had a place to hang a cowboy hat. But she'd rather go back to the fairgrounds than to a restaurant. "Maybe we could go see his racehorses again. Maybe Peter could come too." She paused. "What's a ragamuffin?"

Her mother's hands tightened around Suzy's shoulders. "Where did you hear that?"

"At the party."

"Did Mr. Barrett say it?" She had a funny look on her face and her eyes looked sad.

"No," Suzy said. "It was the mean man with the tie. The one who took the leftover candy canes."

"He's not mean," her mother said. "He's just more comfortable with people who are the same as him."

"But what is a ragamuffin?"

"People who wear rags," her mother said. "But we shouldn't judge people by their clothes. It's how they act that's important."

Suzy nodded. Carl wore rags and he was much nicer than the man with the tie. She pulled away, distracted by the smell of fudge drifting from the kitchen.

"Can I lick the bowl now?" she asked.

CHAPTER SIX

Peter tossed his book bag in a snow bank and scrambled up the side of the dumpster. “No more school!” he shouted, punching his fist in the air and tilting his face toward the sky.

“But there’s school after Christmas vacation,” Suzy said. “Mrs. Roach said so.”

Peter ignored her. He balanced on the edge of the dumpster, pointing his arm and making noises like a machine gun.

“I have to go now,” Suzy said, glancing over her shoulder, relieved Jimmy and Whitey weren’t around.

“You can’t go. I just shot you.”

“My mom told me to come right home,” Suzy said. “After Christmas I can play.” *After Santa comes.*

“Okay,” Peter grumbled. He pivoted, shading his eyes from the sun and staring down at the flat white ground. “This would be a good place to ride your pony,” he said.

“Maybe.” Suzy tugged at her lower lip. “But I don’t want Jimmy to throw snowballs.”

“Nah, I’ll tell him not to.” Peter pointed at a snow-covered bump. “There’s even hay here. Someone in the barns must have thrown it away.”

Suzy dropped her book bag and hurried over to the mysterious mound. She brushed the snow off with her mitten and stared in delight. Peter was right. It was hay.

She tugged at the bale but it was so heavy it only moved a few inches.

Peter jumped down from the dumpster. “What are you doing?”

“I need to take it home,” she said. “So I have hay for Christmas morning.”

Peter kicked the bale with his foot. “It’s too big. You’ll have to pull it on your sled.”

Suzy swallowed. She didn’t have a sled. Sometimes her mother took her sliding on a cardboard box, but that wouldn’t work for pulling hay.

“Don’t you have a sled?” Peter asked. “What about a toboggan? Everyone in town has one of those.”

Suzy stared down at her boots. “I’d rather have a pony than a sled,” she muttered.

Peter was silent for a moment. “You guard the hay,” he said. “And I’ll get my sled and pull it to your house.”

She nodded and plopped down on the hay bale. Peter had already turned and was running toward his house. Little white clouds came from his mouth. He crested the hill and disappeared.

She crossed her arms and waited. And then waited some more. Her toes tingled, like they were being poked with needles, and she stomped her feet. It was always colder when she was alone.

She was glad when Carl trudged around the corner, a dark shape outlined against the snow. A half-filled garbage bag was slung over his back and he had a raggedy scarf wrapped around his neck.

"Hi, Carl," she said.

He frowned. "You should be inside on a day like this."

"I'm waiting for Peter and his sled."

"It's too cold," Carl muttered, pulling his scarf higher over his face. "You both should be inside."

"But we need to take this hay home." Suzy patted the bale. "It's for my pony."

"I didn't know you had a pony."

"Not yet. But Santa's bringing me one for Christmas."

Carl's eyes narrowed and he dropped the garbage bag onto the snow. "Does your mother know? About the pony?"

Suzy shook her head. "She says we can't afford a pet. That's why I need the hay. But my book says ponies don't eat much. Just grass and hay."

"Is that why you took those old buckets?"

"Yes." Suzy nodded happily. "Now I have everything a pony needs."

"But you'll need more than one bale of hay." Carl frowned. "And that hay is moldy. Why do you think they threw it out?"

Suzy rose and peered down at the hay. It looked fine to her, just like the hay she'd fed the racehorse at the barn.

"Besides, a good pony is hard to find," Carl went on. "And a bad one can hurt you. You better ask Santa for something else. Something that's not so much work...or so dangerous."

Suzy's mouth tightened. She sat back down and crossed her arms.

"There must be something else you want," Carl said, after a moment.

"No," she said. "Just a pony."

"What about a doll?"

"I don't like dolls. Ruth Anne's mother calls me a tomboy." Suzy sighed. "I don't think she likes tomboys much."

Carl stepped closer. "But tomboys are great. My daughter was a tomboy. She always liked to get rope. You can build a lot of swings with rope. Why don't you ask Santa for that?"

Suzy perked up. "Rope sounds okay, better than a skipping rope. And I could tie my pony with it. But I can't ask for two presents. And I've already asked for the best thing."

Carl's eyes twinkled and it almost looked like he was smiling beneath his scarf. "Going for broke, are you," he said.

Suzy glanced over her shoulder, checking for Peter. She didn't want to hear anything more about moldy hay or why it wasn't a good idea to ask Santa for a pony. Grownups always acted as if it was a joke, so she didn't like to talk about it. But she'd been planning for her pony for a long time, ever since summer. And her mother said if you were nice to everyone and truly believed, everything always worked out.

She wiggled her feet. Her toes didn't hurt anymore. In fact, she could no longer feel them.

"Probably Peter's mother made him stay inside," Carl said. "Why don't I walk you home? This hay has been here all year. It's not going anywhere."

"You don't think someone else will take it?" she asked.

"No, I don't," Carl said. "And while we're walking I can tell you more about ponies and all the care they need."

"Okay," she said.

She automatically reached for his hand. And even though his glove was ragged, his hand was warm and comforting, and she held it all the way back to her house.

CHAPTER SEVEN

Suzy scooped more snow from the hole, then knelt down and pulled out another handful of frozen grass.

"You must have been digging a long time," Peter said, eyeing the mounds of snow that dotted her yard. "But are you sure your pony will like dead grass?"

"That's what Carl said yesterday." She collected another fistful of grass and carried it toward the shed. "He said wild horses dig through the snow all the time."

"But how much grass do you have?" Peter followed her into the shed. "That doesn't look like much," he said, peering into her bucket.

Suzy trudged back outside. It was difficult working in the snow, and she wished Peter would stop talking and help dig. At least it was warmer today.

"I wasn't allowed to take my sled yesterday," Peter said, "but I'm here now. So we can get that bale by the dumpster."

"No." She shook her head. "Carl said it isn't smart to feed moldy hay. If my pony doesn't have good food, he'll get sick."

"But you only have half a bucket of grass. That won't last until spring. And it's only three days until Christmas."

Suzy's throat turned all tight. There weren't many spots in her yard left to dig, and there wasn't much grass here anyway, even after she'd struggled to push away the snow.

"My dad says only ranchers have horses now," Peter went on. "That they're the only ones who can afford hay because they have more land."

Suzy rubbed her chin with a wet mitten. A blade of precious grass stuck to the wool. She pulled it off, carefully dropped it in her bucket, then squared her shoulders.

"Guess I'll have to find a bigger yard," she said.

Suzy knocked the snow off her plastic shovel, knelt down and triumphantly pulled another handful of grass from the hole. The field by the dumpster was perfect. Nobody ever cut the grass here.

Peter had wandered off long ago but he'd left his sled, and it was now almost half full. More than enough for a little pony.

A shadow darkened the snow. She shaded her eyes and peered up.

"Hi, Carl," she said, reaching back and pulling out another bunch of grass. It was easier to work without mittens but her fingers froze so it was necessary to put her mittens back on every few minutes and warm her hands.

"What the heck are you doing?"

She rubbed her fingers, blinking in surprise. Carl sounded different, disapproving—almost like a regular adult.

"Picking grass for my pony," she said.

"But I told you range horses do that to survive. I didn't mean that you should do it."

"Why not?" She pulled her mittens back on and wiggled her stiff fingers.

"It's too much work," Carl said. "People don't have time to dig through the snow. There are lots of other reasons too." He went on to talk about nutrition and colic and practicality, but Suzy found it hard to listen.

Scraping away the snow might be too much work for grownups, but she had lots of time after school. And now that she'd found the grass by the dumpster, it would be easy to gather food. In the spring when the snow melted, it would be even easier.

She smiled up at Carl, pulled off her mittens and laid them in the snow, then reached down for another handful of grass.

Carl didn't say anything else. He just stood stock still, blocking the sun, watching her work. One of his boots had a hole in the toe where the tip of a gray sock poked through. Like her, he was probably glad it was warmer today.

"You're as stubborn as me," he finally said. He huffed for a moment, then picked up her shovel and scooped aside some snow. He seemed to know where to dig because there was way more grass at the bottom of his hole.

"You're a good digger, Carl," she said happily.

"Move your sled closer and I'll load it up," he muttered.

"It's not my sled. It's Peter's. But he promised to let me use it this winter."

"You play with those boys? After all those times when they pushed you in the snow?"

She shrugged. That seemed a long time ago. And even Jimmy didn't throw snowballs at her anymore. She was glad she hadn't tattled, especially on Peter.

"My mom says it doesn't do people any good to stay angry," she said. "And that Santa wants everyone to be friends." She tugged her mittens back on and studied the sled. It was so full some of the grass had fallen off. "Looks like I have enough food now," she said, with utter satisfaction.

"But what makes you so certain Santa will bring a pony?" Carl asked.

"Why wouldn't he?"

"Well," Carl said, "we don't always get what we want. And it's hard for Santa to fit everything on his sleigh. Maybe you should ask for something easier, like a turkey dinner."

"My mother already bought a turkey," Suzy said happily. "It's so big I'm allowed to have a second helping."

Carl sighed and picked up the frayed rope attached to the sled. "Want some help pulling this home?"

"No, thanks. I better do it." She wrapped her hand around the rope. "I need to get used to pulling the grass all by myself."

CHAPTER EIGHT

"I see you were playing in the yard yesterday," Suzy's mother said. "Were you building a snowman? Or making a fort?"

Suzy pulled her soup bowl closer and picked up her spoon. "Just digging holes," she said, not looking at her mother. "And playing with Peter's sled."

"Wouldn't it be great if Santa brought you a sled?" her mother asked. She sat down at the table and buttered several crackers.

"That would be a nice present from you," Suzy said, blowing on the hot soup. "But not from Santa."

"What do you want Santa to bring?"

"I already told him." Suzy bit into the crunchy cracker. "We wrote letters in school. So he'd have time to prepare."

"Maybe you should write another letter and leave it tomorrow night. I can help."

Suzy wiggled on the chair. She didn't want her mother to know she'd asked Santa for a pony. She might be like Carl and say children shouldn't ask for something like that.

"It's important to dream big," Suzy's mother went on. "And Santa wants you to be happy. But sometimes it takes a long time to fill every wish."

Suzy nodded in understanding. She'd wanted a pony for as long as she could remember.

The phone rang and Suzy's mother rose so fast her chair tipped. When she answered she sounded out of breath.

Suzy grabbed two crackers, broke them into little pieces and quickly added them to her bowl. It wasn't ladylike to put crackers in her soup. But lately her mother had been distracted and talking on the phone a lot. She knew it wasn't Mrs. Roach calling because her mother sounded too happy.

She spoke on the phone for a long time and when she hung up Suzy had almost finished her soup.

"Mr. Barrett says hello," her mother said with a smile. "He sent you a Christmas present."

Suzy dropped her spoon. Mr. Barrett had sent some pretty red flowers to her mother, but she didn't know he'd also left a present.

"Where is it?" she asked.

"It's in the closet. You can put it under the tree now."

Suzy scrambled from her chair and pulled open the closet door. The present was on the floor, a big mysterious box wrapped in the prettiest paper she'd ever seen. It had smiling snowmen and bright lights and Christmas trees, and it was even topped with a store-bought bow.

"What do you think it is?" She dropped to her knees and pressed her nose against the box.

"You'll find out on Christmas morning," her mother said, still smiling.

Suzy took another sniff. She was certain she could smell peppermint. Maybe Mr. Barrett hadn't forgotten and the leftover candy canes were in the box. Carl said horses liked peppermints as much as sugar. She could give a candy cane to her pony and another one to Carl. She had a feeling Carl didn't get much for Christmas. No wonder those men thought he might starve.

"No peeking," her mother said.

"I hope it's candy canes," Suzy said, looking up at her mom. "And I hope Carl has some turkey to eat this year... Maybe we could invite him?"

"Invite Carl?" Her mother blinked. "For Christmas dinner?"

Suzy nodded. "We have a big turkey. And you said there would be enough for seconds."

"But Christmas is a time for family and friends."

"Carl is my friend." Suzy clutched the box. "And he has no family. He lives alone in a barn. And he's hungry and hasn't had turkey for a long time. *That's* what he wants for Christmas."

Her mother was quiet for a moment, but her eyes turned all shiny. When she spoke her voice sounded funny. “You’re absolutely right,” she said. “We should invite him.”

“I’ll go tell him,” Suzy said.

“And maybe I better write a note.”

“Like a proper invitation?” Suzy asked. “For special guests?”

Suzy’s mother nodded. “Exactly,” she said.

CHAPTER NINE

"I'm going to have so much grass." Suzy stared delightedly at the sled. Carl was a big help. He knew where to dig for the tallest grass and even better, he knew what kinds of food might make a pony sick.

"Thank you, Carl," she added. "You're way more help than Peter. And now I know a lot more about ponies."

Carl rose and dumped another armful of brown grass onto the sled. "So now do you understand why a pony is too much work? And how they need other things besides food?"

"Yes." Suzy nodded. "Like tack. That's why I won't expect a saddle. I'll ride my pony bareback and ask for a saddle next Christmas."

Carl rolled his eyes and looked at the sky. "If wishes were horses," he said, "all beggars would ride."

"What does that mean?"

"Just that you can't always get what you want."

"I know," Suzy said. "Sometimes you have to wait a very long time."

Carl sighed. "Picking grass is probably a waste of time. But I suppose I can help you again tomorrow."

"I can't come tomorrow." Suzy rose and wiped the snow off her mittens. "That's the day before Christmas and I'm helping make dessert. And I'm going to cut up a paper bag and wrap Mommy's present too."

Carl nodded but his smile looked rather sad. "Of course. Have a real nice Christmas, Suzy."

"Oh, I almost forgot. You're invited for Christmas dinner. And I can show you my pony then too."

"You're a sweet girl," he said, "and I appreciate the thought. But Christmas is for family. Your mother would be shocked if I knocked at your door."

"No, she wouldn't." Suzy dropped her mitten and fumbled in her pocket for the note. The paper was a little damp where snow had seeped through her jacket, but it was written in her mother's special writing. And at the bottom Suzy had added a picture of the three of them sitting at the table. She'd even colored the turkey with her favorite crayon.

"The turkey won't really be purple," she said, passing him the note. "But I think it looks pretty, don't you?"

Carl stared down at the invitation for so long she wondered if he could read. And his eyes were blinking as though he had trouble seeing.

"It's easier to read printing," she added helpfully. "But my mother always forgets and writes her words."

Carl turned away. He seemed to be wiping snow off his face and didn't speak for a long time. When he turned around, he was still blinking. "I'd be honored to come for Christmas dinner," he said.

"That's good." Suzy scooped up the rope, her mind filled with thoughts of turkey and candy canes and ponies. "Because I think it's going to be the best Christmas ever."

"I do too," Carl said.

CHAPTER TEN

Suzy studied their Christmas tree, admiring the angel perched at the top. Her hair was white and her dress was gold and she was so beautiful. Everything on the tree was perfect, and the room smelled like popcorn and pine and peppermint.

A pony ornament dangled from a lower branch, and she stroked it with her finger. Last year she'd asked for a pony but Santa hadn't realized she meant a real one. He'd left a wooden ornament instead. But this year she was older and knew it was important to be very clear.

She still loved her little ornament though. Like the angel, he was too beautiful to be real. His body was gold but his mane and tail were white. She squeezed her eyes shut and made a fervent wish. She didn't care what color her pony was—she just wanted one.

She ran across the room, past the two dangling stockings, and pressed her nose against the cold window. Snow gleamed in the backyard, and by contrast, the shed looked dark and rather lonely. But inside the shed, everything was ready.

Grass was carefully piled, along with the two shriveled carrots and a bucket of water. She hadn't been allowed to take any of the expensive sugar lumps her mother had bought yesterday, but Suzy had shoveled all afternoon and made a welcoming path for her pony. The shed door was propped open with her shovel too, because there were a lot of houses and she guessed Santa would be in a hurry.

She sighed, her breath frosting the glass. It was going to be impossible to sleep tonight but staring at the dark shed wouldn't make Santa come any faster. She turned and hurried back to the tree, deciding to count her presents again.

This year, she had three: two from her mother and one from Mr. Barrett.

She picked up the gift from Mr. Barrett. It still smelled like peppermint and it thumped when she shook it, so heavy it felt like five candy canes—or at least four. Last Christmas, she only had one candy cane, and she was so delighted with her good fortune, she wiggled with delight.

"Suzy, are you peeking?"

"No, Mom." Suzy quickly pushed the present back under the tree. "But I know it's candy canes. And I'm going to give one to Carl when he comes tomorrow. He really likes them, and I'll have so many. It's easier to share when you have a lot."

Her mother laughed. "It's definitely easier."

But then her mother's smile faded. She knelt beside the tree and gripped Suzy's hand. "It might not be candy canes though. Don't be disappointed if it's not what you expect. Remember, this isn't just about Santa and presents. If you can make someone else happy on Christmas Day, that's a nice feeling too."

Suzy nodded, pretending to listen, but her mother always talked about how Santa could only bring appropriate gifts. Last year, Suzy didn't even know what 'appropriate' meant, but this year she was bigger and knew a lot more. She'd picked grass and found buckets and even cleaned out the shed. And she'd tried to be really, really good.

She wiggled her hand, impatient for her mother to stop talking.

"So you understand?" her mother finally said. "It's good to hope and believe and work for things, but sometimes they don't come as quickly as we want."

"But I've been good, right?" Suzy asked.

Her mother nodded. "Yes. You've been very good."

Relief filled Suzy, warming her like a cup of hot chocolate. If her mother thought she was good, surely Santa would too.

"We better go to bed now," Suzy said. "So we're asleep when he comes."

CHAPTER ELEVEN

"Merry Christmas!"

Suzy sat up and sleepily rubbed her eyes. Her mother stood in the doorway, smiling. "Let's go down and see if Santa came," her mother added.

"Is it morning?" Suzy scrambled from the bed, almost falling over the blankets in her haste. She rushed to the window and stared out, straining to see the shed and Santa's tracks. But it was hard to see anything from this angle.

She charged from her room and down the steps, passing her mother at the bottom of the stairs.

Wide awake now, she yanked on her boots and grabbed her jacket.

Her mother frowned. "Where are you going? Let's check our stockings."

"I have to go outside first," Suzy said, so excited she could barely speak.

She flung open the door and rushed from the house, running along the newly dug path. The shed door was open, and she slowed her steps. Carl said horses were easily surprised and she didn't want to scare her pony on the very first day.

"Hi, pony," she called. She eased to a stop and stared into the shed, her heart pounding.

She blinked and stared some more. And then it felt like her chest was going to explode. The grass was there, the carrots too. But there was no pony.

She crumpled in the doorway, her hands pressed into the cold snow. The shed was empty, truly empty. Nothing had changed except that the water in the bucket was frozen.

Snow crunched and she glanced around. Her mother had followed her out, not even bothering to put on a coat.

And then Suzy realized what had happened. *He* hadn't come! She scrambled to her feet and grabbed her mother's hand. "We need to go back inside," she said urgently. "Back to bed. Santa hasn't come yet."

"Oh, honey," her mother whispered. She didn't say anything more, just scooped Suzy up and carried her inside. And then she just held her, squeezing so tightly Suzy could barely breathe.

"I think Santa did come," her mother said, finally putting her down. "Let's go see what nice surprises he left." She pulled off Suzy's boots and then her jacket.

Suzy stared numbly at the Christmas tree. There were more presents and the stockings bulged. So Santa had been here. He just hadn't brought her what she wanted. Again.

She rubbed at her hot eyes. "But I asked for a p-pony."

"We talked about that," her mother said gently. "And you know Santa can't bring little children ponies. They're not big enough to look after them."

"But I can. I've been practicing all year. And Carl said I know a lot."

"But Santa doesn't bring presents like that. There wouldn't be room for other children's gifts. You wouldn't want that, would you?"

Suzy sniffed. "But he brought Ruth Anne's sister a piano last year. And that's even bigger than a pony."

"You should be happy with whatever he brings," her mother said. "Some people don't get anything for Christmas. Now I don't want to hear anything more about ponies."

She tugged Suzy toward the tree. "Look what Santa brought!" She spoke in the excited voice that grownups use when they're pretending to be happy.

Suzy stumbled toward the tree, pressing her lips together so hard they hurt. She wanted to complain about Santa some more, but she could tell her mother was sad too. Maybe she didn't get what she wanted for Christmas either.

"Oh, look!" her mother said, still speaking in that high fake voice. "A sled. Isn't that great!"

Suzy slowly picked up the rope attached to a shiny red sled. It looked brand new and it had wooden sides and would be good for pulling grass. But then she remembered she didn't need to dig for grass anymore. And her lower lip quivered.

"Let's see what's in your stocking," her mother went on, lifting it off the nail on the mantle. "Is that a horse head sticking out?"

Suzy brightened and pulled out the horse. It turned out to be a long pencil with a brown horse on the top. The horse had a red hat with a bell, and it jingled when it moved. "This is my favorite present," she said.

"Maybe you can draw Carl a picture with it," her mother said. "And give it to him when he comes."

"But I'm giving him a candy cane," Suzy said. "He'd like something to eat more than anything else. And I don't think he has a fridge to put pictures on." She reached under the tree for Mr. Barrett's present. "Can I open this now? Before breakfast?"

At her mother's nod, Suzy ripped open the paper. The smell of peppermint grew stronger. The box was even bigger than the one at the party and her stomach turned all fluttery. There might even be ten candy canes inside.

She yanked the lid from the box and for a moment could only stare. There was just one candy cane, but it was the biggest and best she'd ever seen. Maybe even the biggest in the whole world. It was thicker than the handle of her shovel, and it wasn't just red and white. It was green too.

"Mr. Barrett sure is a nice man," Suzy said. "He must have remembered what he said at the party."

"He is nice," her mother said. "And I know he felt bad that you didn't get the leftover candy canes." Her cheeks were pink and flushed, and she looked happy too.

Suzy ran her hand over the enormous candy cane. It might last until summer if she only sucked it. She pressed it to her chest, scarcely able to imagine having candy every day. "Can I take it to school and show it to Ruth Anne?"

"Sure," her mother said. "It's your candy cane. You can do whatever you want."

Suzy cradled the giant candy cane in her arms. It reached from the top of her shoulder to her waist. It was much better than any doll. Better even than ten little candy canes.

And then she stiffened. "But now I don't have a candy cane to give Carl."

"He's coming for dinner," her mother said, rising and walking toward the kitchen. "I don't think he'll expect a present."

Suzy's hands tightened around Mr. Barrett's gift. Carl probably didn't expect a present. But last week he'd looked so happy when she gave him the candy cane. And she knew what it was like to be disappointed in Santa. Mr. Barrett's present had helped her feel better, and she still had two presents from her mother to open.

But Carl didn't have anyone else to make him feel better—only her.

CHAPTER TWELVE

"Everything looks so pretty," Suzy said, carefully folding a third napkin and placing it beside the fork. She'd set the table almost entirely by herself, even remembering where to put the glasses.

"Do you think Carl will want water or milk?" she asked, scampering to the fridge.

"Why don't you wait and ask him," her mother said. "He should be here soon. Are you sure he's coming?"

Suzy nodded and hurried back to the table. She couldn't wait to eat. The whole house smelled like turkey and her mother always made the best gravy—brown, thick and delicious.

"Carl can have my dressing," she said. "And that red stuff too."

"It's called cranberry." Her mother stopped mashing the potatoes and tilted her head. "I didn't think you liked dressing."

Suzy shrugged. She couldn't remember if she liked dressing or not, but she absolutely loved turkey and gravy. It would be fine if that was the only food on her plate. She climbed onto her chair and glanced toward the door.

"I wish Carl would come now," she said.

"Sometimes it's hard to go to someone else's house," her mother said, "especially if you haven't been around people for a while. We'll have to understand if he isn't able to join us. Maybe we could save some food for later."

"But I have to give him his present." Suzy's eyes shot to the brightly colored box. It had taken a long time to rewrap the giant candy cane. And she was eager to see Carl's face, especially since she'd drawn a picture of them picking grass and taped it to the top.

She wiggled in her chair, almost as excited as when she'd woken this morning—before she ran to the shed and discovered there was no pony.

She blew out a sigh. At least now she had her own sled. Santa probably left it because he wanted her to gather more grass. Maybe he thought she didn't have enough for a pony to eat.

But she would pick grass all year and fill the shed before next Christmas. And she'd print a longer letter—maybe even mail it in the summer—and tell Santa that she was still being good and that she was truly ready for a pony.

Her mother must have heard Suzy's sigh. She untied her apron and walked over to the table. "Are you sure you want to give away your candy cane?"

Suzy nodded. "Mr. Barrett knows it makes people happy when he gives away things. So I don't think he'll mind if I do too."

"I don't think he'll mind either." Her mother's cheeks turned red, like they did whenever she talked about Mr. Barrett. But even though she was smiling, her eyes were all watery. "It's nice how you think of others—"

She stopped talking and wrapped Suzy in a big hug, the really long kind. "I'm proud of you," she whispered. Her breath tickled Suzy's ear and it was hard not to wiggle. And then there was a knock on the door and her mother straightened.

"It's Carl!" Suzy said, scrambling from the chair.

She scooped up the box and ran to the door. But it was impossible to turn the knob with one hand and she didn't want to put down Carl's present. Her mother reached over her head to help.

Suzy gripped the box tightly to her chest. "He's going to be so surprised," she whispered, excited to see his face when he opened the present.

Her mother wiped her eyes and smiled, then swung open the door.

Carl stood on the walkway. "Merry Christmas," he said. He ducked his head and looked rather shy, and his tattered sleeve hung down over his glove.

"Merry Christmas," Suzy and her mother both said.

Suzy reached out to tug him inside and give him his present. But he pressed a brown rope between her fingers then stepped sideways. And she could only stare in shock.

A pony stared back at her. His eyes were big and brown, his mane was white and his body was golden. In fact, he was the same color as the wooden pony on their Christmas tree—he had to be the most beautiful pony in the world. And she was sure he was alive because white breath came from his nose and when he moved, his forelock fell over his curious eyes.

"I found him in the barn this morning," Carl said gruffly. "Santa must have thought it was a better place for him to stay. Until you have things ready here."

Suzy's entire body turned numb and Carl's present dropped from her hands into the snow. It was impossible to breathe and her heart thumped like a drum. *Santa had brought her a pony after all!* She couldn't speak. Could only stand and stare.

"He's a good pony," Carl went on. "Safe and gentle with children. I hope it's all right with you, ma'am," he cleared his throat, "but I've never met anybody who wanted a pony more."

Suzy looked up. Her mother had her hands pressed over her mouth and her eyes were watery again. "But we can't afford—"

"With your permission, ma'am," Carl said, "I've arranged to have hay delivered. You won't have to worry about anything."

A squeak of joy escaped from Suzy's mouth and she was finally able to move. She shot forward and wrapped her arms around the pony's neck. He was solid yet cuddly, his velvety body so warm it felt like he was hugging her back. And she didn't want to ever let go.

"What's his name?" she finally managed.

"I believe Santa called him Prince," Carl said, "but you can call him whatever you want."

"That's a great name," Suzy said. She pried her arms off his neck but kept her fingers entwined in his silky mane and inspected him all over. Sunlight glinted off his body, making him look bathed in gold. In fact the entire yard looked shinier, now that Prince was in it.

She stared for another moment. Then she dropped the rope and hugged Carl. "Thank you for bringing him," she whispered.

She turned back to the pony, squeezing the rope, still scarcely able to believe.

"Suzy, put this on," her mother said, holding out her jacket. "I think dinner will be a little late this year."

She waited while her mother bent and tugged up the zipper. And it was obvious she was just as stunned about the pony because she completely forgot to bring Suzy a hat or mittens.

"But I don't understand," her mother said, looking up at Carl, her hands still clutching Suzy's jacket.

Suzy fidgeted, impatient to get back to Prince. She wanted to feed him the grass in the shed, then climb on his back and ride over to Peter's.

"I've been a stubborn fool," Carl said. "Hanging on to old hurts. But I talked to my son yesterday. And I realize I can't keep blaming him for an accident that wasn't his fault." He cleared his throat and looked down at Suzy.

Suzy smiled up at him, glad to hear that Carl had family after all.

"Who's your son?" Suzy's mother asked, still fiddling with Suzy's hood. "Does he live around here?"

"About twenty miles from town," Carl said. "Before the accident he loved to train Thoroughbreds. And his little sister loved to gallop them."

They all turned as a blue truck rumbled up in front of the house. Mr. Barrett stepped out. He scooped up two bales of hay from the back of his truck, tucked them under his arms and strode up the walkway.

He dropped them on the snow and stared at Carl, then stepped forward and hugged him, just like Suzy had, only much longer.

And then he did a very odd thing. He turned to Suzy's mother and kissed her on the lips. But she didn't seem to mind, even though she'd told Suzy that kissing was only for grownups who loved each other.

Then Mr. Barrett knelt in front of Suzy. "I should have realized you were the little girl with the generous heart," he said. His eyes were all blue and glittery—even bluer than Carl's—and his voice sounded a little rusty. "You gave me back my father."

Suzy scrunched her nose, not sure what he was talking about. She was silent for a moment, then pointed at Prince. "And Santa gave me a pony. Want to come with me and Carl, and feed Prince the grass we picked?"

"I'd like that," Mr. Barrett said. "Very much. And if you want to ride later, I brought a little saddle. It was...my sister's. I'm sure it will be a perfect fit."

A saddle too! Suzy smiled. She gripped Prince's rope in one hand and reached for Carl's hand with the other. They waited while Mr. Barrett picked up the hay, then they turned and together followed the pathway to the shed. It was so narrow Prince barely fit.

Suzy peered up at Carl. "I shoveled a long time," she said, "but maybe I should have made the path wider. I hope Prince likes it here."

"I know he will," Carl said. "We'll make sure of that."

And for some reason Carl didn't look so old anymore. He smiled over his shoulder at Mr. Barrett, and Mr. Barrett grinned back. Even Prince looked happy. He didn't seem to mind the narrow path. His ears were pricked and he had a bounce in his walk, as if excited to see his new home.

They filed into the shed. Prince immediately stuck his nose in the mound of grass and began to eat while Carl and Mr. Barrett started talking about the best place to build a stall. Mr. Barrett wanted to build a bigger shed and Carl suggested they add a hayloft. They poked at the walls and measured the floor, and neither of the men seemed in any hurry to stop talking.

And then Suzy remembered she hadn't even given Carl his present yet. She ran back to the front door and scooped the box from the snow just as her mother hurried from the house.

At first Suzy was afraid it was time for dinner. However, her mother was buttoning her coat and even wore her best boots. She clutched the precious box of sugar cubes and her face glowed, so it was obvious she was just excited about Prince.

Seeing her mother's eyes sparkle like that made Suzy feel so light she thought she might float over the snow, and she was doubly grateful to Santa for making it all happen. It didn't seem right to ask for anything else—not this Christmas—but she couldn't help wanting everyone to be as happy as her and her mom.

"Carl and Mr. Bartlett sure like to talk a lot," she whispered, glancing toward Prince's shed and the steady rumble of their voices. "Do you think we could set another place at the table?" She crossed her fingers. "For Mr. Bartlett?"

Her mother smiled and rumpled Suzy's hair. "I already have," she said.

***

ABOUT THE AUTHOR

Bev Pettersen is a three-time nominee in the National Readers Choice Award as well as a two-time finalist in the Romance Writers of America's Golden Heart® Contest. She competed for five years on the Alberta Thoroughbred race circuit and is an Equine Canada certified coach. She lives in Nova Scotia with her family and when not writing novels, she's riding.
Visit her at http://www.bevpettersen.com

Made in the USA
Middletown, DE
04 January 2017